THE NEW ADVENTURES OF MR TOAD

TOAD in TROUBLED Waters

Tom Moorhouse
with pictures by Holly Swain

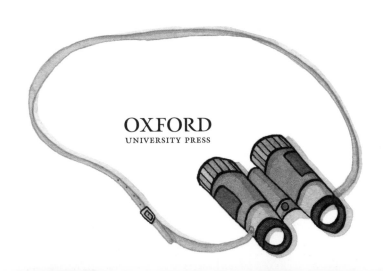

OXFORD
UNIVERSITY PRESS

Contents

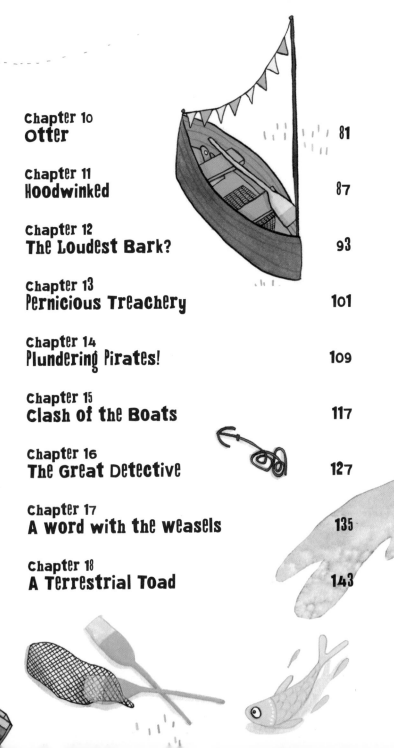

Toad's Preparatory Notes for Jolly and Successful River Boaty Experiences

(Teejay's too, when Mr T wasn't looking) ⟶ **by Toad**

Dear Old Ratty used to say there is nothing half so much worth doing as messing about in boats—especially if one's boat is the swiftest of modern speedboats.

Oh, is he prepared this time?

Before embarking on his aquatic forays, the intelligent and well-prepared Toad has assembled the following notes on the river and its folk . . .

The River

And fish! Ratty is taking us fishing. I want to catch a shark.

Big, wide, and deep. Home to diverse animals, ducks, water rats, and what-have-you. Not to be entered without suitable attire.

Mr Toad

Now rescued from his ice house, in which he was incarcerated for a century by devious weasels, Toad is set for adventure. With his trusty copy of *Wild Wood and Water,* he shall live the life nautical! Splice the mainsail, weigh anchor, and set course! Toot-toot!

I don't know what this is.

Teejay, Ratty, and Mo

Ooh, I like being gallant and noble. Badge says I'm a pest.

My gallant and noble rescuers. Teejay is a Toad, so naturally a fine youngster. Ratty is a natural boating type; some high opinions but a fine fellow. Mo is my go-to Mole for newfangled gadgety objects.

7

Badge. She's
lovely, really!

Ms Badger

Extremely fierce lady. Holder
and enforcer of an unfairly
restrictive list of banned
activities. Like water
dragons, leviathans,
and giant squid – to be
avoided if spotted!

Badge says her list is the
only thing between Mr Toad
and disaster.

otter

I believe him to be the
grandson of *my* good
Otter. Elusive
fellow, keeps to
his narrowboat.
Well respected
hereabouts. Fond
of fish. Apt to be
argumentative,
I advise caution.

Mr and Mrs Rat

They're nice, and they make cake too.

Salt of the earth boating folks. Parents of Ratty. Charming little waterside place, with own moorings. Excellent tea and coffee making facilities. Must visit soon.

Chief Executive Weasel and Mr Ripton

Mr T says they are blights upon Animalkind and should be hoisted by their own petards. I don't know what a petard is.

Weasel chief and his villainous aide. Thankfully not river types, and so unlikely to be encountered. (But if I do see them they shall receive a soaking, make no mistake.)

Hehee! Wet weasels, soggy stoats!

9

Chapter 1
Gone fishing

Teejay stared at her fishing line. Nothing, not even a ripple. The river lazed by. Insects hummed in the shade beneath the trees. And Teejay sighed. 'Anyone caught anything yet?'

Ratty yawned and stretched. 'Nope. How about you, Mo?'

Mo lay on his back in the grass. He snored.

'I think that's a "no",' said Ratty.

Teejay shook her fishing rod. 'Come

on, fish, do something!' She scowled at the water. 'We've been here ages.'

'You've got to wait,' said Ratty. 'Dad says that's half the fun.'

'Your dad's got a strange idea of fun.'

Ratty grinned. 'Don't worry. The riverbank's never boring for long.'

'Tell the fish that,' said Teejay, glumly. '*They're* boring.'

Ratty leaned back against a tree. He pulled his baseball cap over his eyes. 'Just enjoy the quiet.'

'I can't,' said Teejay. 'Toads don't like quiet.' She watched the river, wishing that something, anything, would happen.

Pitterpatterpitterpatterpitterpatter.

Teejay blinked. 'Rat, can you hear something?'

'Yes. There's this person who won't stop talking—'

'Not me, you twit. Something else.'

Pitterpatterpitterpatterpitterpatter.

snore snore

'There it is again.' Teejay sat
up. 'Rat, something's coming!'

Pitterpatterpitterpatter!

A hare hurtled into view, dashing through
the trees. He spied Teejay and skidded to a
stop. 'Warning! Warning!' panted the hare.
'It's coming! Clear the river, it's coming!'

Ratty got to his feet. 'What's coming?'

'No time, more folks to tell. Be
warned, get back, take cover!'
And the hare sprinted away down
the river.

Teejay stared after the hare. 'Does that happen often?'

'No, not really,' said Ratty.

'Hey!' a voice shouted from the river. 'Hey, hey!'

Teejay spun around to see two bank voles in a canoe, paddling frantically downstream. 'Don't just stand there, run for it!' cried the first bank vole. 'He's back on the water!'

'Who's on the water?' called Teejay.

'That maniac, that's who!' shouted the second vole. 'He's going to flood our camp again! Now get away! Leg it!'

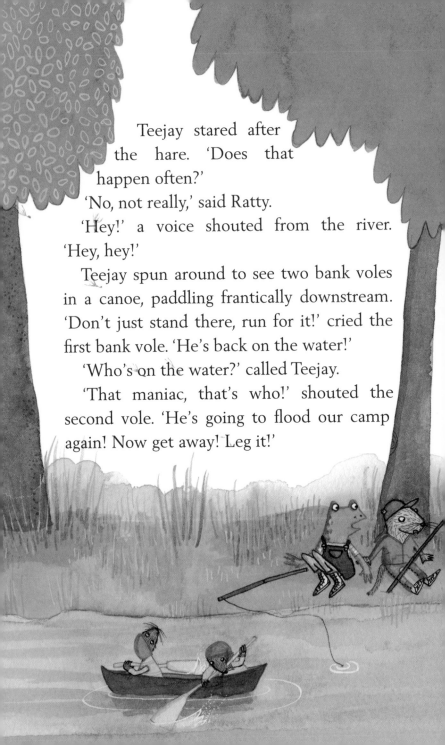

They shot by, still paddling like crazy, and disappeared around the bend.

'This is really weird,' said Ratty.

'And getting weirder,' said Teejay. 'Look!'

Quacking filled the air. A gaggle of ducks flapped and splashed towards them. 'It'll get us, it'll get us!' cried the ducks, as they shot past. 'No dibbling! No dabbling! Swim, swim, swim for your lives!'

And then they too were gone.

'This river,' said Teejay, 'has gone bonkers. What's going on?'

Ratty shook his head. 'I don't know. This has never happened before.'

'Right, we'd better wake Mo up.'

But before Teejay could move, a low rumble echoed through the trees.

RRRRUUM-vRRuUMMM-BRRuRRR-vRRRUMMM . . .

'Now what?' Teejay glanced at Ratty. 'Thunder?'

The ground trembled. Ratty's whiskers quivered. 'No,' he said. 'It's coming from the water.'

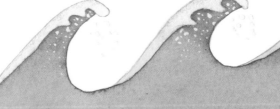

. . . RRRRUUM-vRRuUMMM-BRRuRRR-vRRRUMMM . . .

He shouted over the roar, 'And it's *really big.*'

chapter 2
Sploosh!

Rrruum-vRruummm-BRRuRRR-vRRRummm . . . A massive
speedboat powered into view. It swerved from
side to side down the river, sending water
sloshing against the banks.

'Too fast!' cried Ratty. 'It's going *way* too
fast!'

. . . mmwwwRRRRRAAAAAARRRuuummmm!
The boat screamed past. Teejay clutched
at her ears. 'Ow, and too loud!' she yelled.
Through the dark window Teejay glimpsed a
figure, hunched over the wheel. Then the boat

19

veered around the bend and roared away. And in its wake a huge wave surged.

'Oh no!' yelled Ratty. 'Run!'

The wave swept towards them. Teejay scrambled back from the river's edge.

Splooooosh!

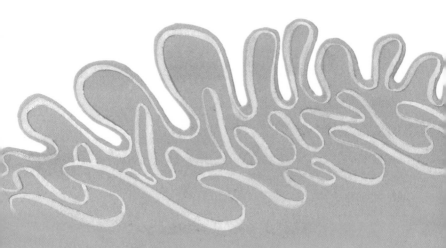

Cold water splashed up her legs. 'Ugh!' said Teejay. 'My feet are wet.'

Ratty took off his trainers and emptied them out. He glared after the boat. 'Somebody,' he said, 'is going to pay for this.'

'W-w-what h-h-happened?'

It was Mo's voice. Teejay and Ratty dashed to his side. He was sitting in a puddle, eyes tight closed. Water streamed from his fur and clothes. It dripped off his nose and glasses.

'Ooh,' said Ratty, 'that's a nasty way to wake up.'

'It went right over him! Poor Mo, are you OK?' said Teejay.

'N-no,' said Mo. 'I'm c-c-cold. And my legs feel jumpy.'

21

'Yep,' said Ratty. 'There's a reason for that.'

Teejay blinked. 'Mo, I don't want you to panic, but there's a fish on your trousers.'

An angry-looking carp was bouncing in Mo's lap.

Mo kept his eyes shut. 'Please get it off.'

'Hang on.' Ratty scooped the fish into the water. It flipped its tail and swam away.

Mo got to his feet. He sniffed and wiped

his glasses. 'I-I don't think I like fishing very much.'

'At least you caught something,' said Teejay, brightly.

Crash! Crunch!

'What was that?' said Mo.

'That,' said Ratty, 'sounded like a really big boat hitting the riverbank.'

'Oh.' Mo thought for a moment. 'Good.'

'Come on, let's go and see,' said Teejay. 'They might need our help!'

Chapter 3
Nautical coves

Teejay sprinted down the riverbank, with Ratty and Mo just behind. Through the trees she glimpsed a huge, white shape.

'I can see it,' she panted, 'we're nearly there!'

They ran out into a grassy field. In front of them was the boat, white and sleek and massive.

'Wow,' said Teejay. 'Whoever owns that must be rich.'

'And a *really* bad driver,' said Ratty. 'What a mess!'

The boat had rammed into the riverbank

so hard its nose was stuck in the grass. It was covered in scrapes, and bits of smashed wood floated in the water around it. The words 'Little Portly' were painted on the prow, but the letters were scratched.

'But who'd buy an expensive boat if they can't drive it?' said Mo.

'Ahoy there, me landlubbery chaps!' cried a voice. A hatch opened, and a short figure bounded onto the deck.

CRASH!
CRUNCH!

Ratty put his head in his paws. 'There's your answer.'

On the deck stood Mr Toad, splendid in a white sailing outfit. He wore a sailor's hat and a handkerchief knotted around his neck.

He raised a telescope to his eye. 'By Neptune, I spy seafaring coves! All aboard, there!'

He threw down a small ladder, and Teejay, Ratty, and Mo scrambled up.

'All hands hoay, ye scallywags!' cried Mr Toad.

'Hello, Mr T,' said Teejay. 'Why are you talking like that?'

'All ships' captains speak this way.' Mr Toad waved a hand. 'It's what one does on the river.'

'You're not on the river,' said Ratty. 'You're mostly in the field.'

Mr Toad gave him a stern look. 'My good vessel may indeed have run aground,' he said, 'but it's nothing a skilled sailor can't put right.'

'That's good,' said Mo. 'Do you know one?'

'As it happens,' said Mr Toad, 'I am the finest sailor in these parts! Anyhow what happened to your clothes? D'you fall in?'

'No, *you* drenched me with your boat!'

'Are you sure it was me?'

'Yes.'

'Well, what's a little damp to a brave chap like

you, eh?' Mr Toad clapped Mo on the shoulder. 'Especially when there are mysteries to solve and clues to unpuzzle!'

'Did you say "clues", Mr T?' said Teejay.

'I certainly did.' Mr Toad held a finger in the air. 'For I have embarked upon a nautical mission of paramount importance!'

'Gosh,' said Teejay.

'I was seeking the next clue when I had this little mishap,' Mr Toad continued. He lowered his voice to a whisper. 'It's close. We're on its trail.'

Teejay peered out at the clearing. 'I can't see any clues.'

'But that's the brilliance of it! They could be anything.' Mr Toad pulled a round object from under a bench and gave it to her. 'Just look at this one.'

'Mr Toad,' said Mo, carefully, 'are you sure that's a clue?'

'Because you just gave her a turnip,' said Ratty.

Mr Toad grinned. 'Turn it over, Toad Junior!'

Teejay turned the turnip over. 'Hey, it's hollow!'

She reached in and pulled out a plastic tag. It read:

I lie between a pair of piers. You can't see me for the trees. 51° 33' 50" N 0° 45' 17" W

'You see?' said Mr Toad. 'They're disguised. Solve the riddle, and it takes you to the next clue.'

Teejay frowned at it. 'What are those funny numbers?'

'That's the magic code,' said Mr Toad.

'Oh, they're co-ordinates,' said Ratty. 'You use them to look up places on a map.'

'Maps? Pah! Bunch of old-fashioned papery piffle. Can't be doing with 'em,' said Mr Toad. He leapt over to a large screen on the instrument panel. 'Not when I have my miraculous code-pointing-clue-finder.'

Mo rushed to the screen. 'Oh,' he squeaked, 'that's a satnav! It's *wonderful!*'

Teejay peered over Mo's shoulder. The screen showed a perfect map of the river, complete with houses, trees, and fields. In the centre was Mr Toad's boat, the front half on the riverbank and a blue arrow bouncing up and down in front of it.

'I tap in the magic code and drive to where the arrow points me,' grinned Mr Toad. 'It's foolproof. I mostly don't even bother to look out of the window.'

31

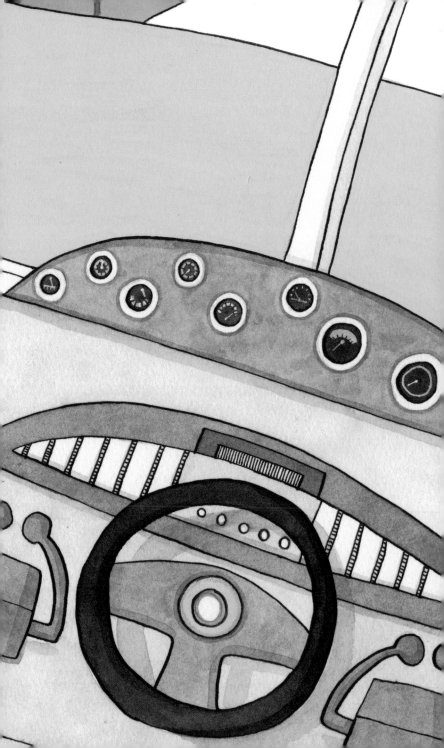

'And that's why you're stuck in the riverbank,' said Ratty.

Mo tapped the screen. 'This says that the clue's right in front of us.'

'Ooh, can we try to find it?' said Teejay. 'Go on, Mr T, I bet we can!'

Mr Toad smiled. 'Absolutely! Come on, last one to solve the puzzle's a stinker!'

Chapter 4
PierPeering Round the clearing

Teejay grabbed the clue-tag. 'OK, so we're looking for two piers. Can anyone see them?'

'We should be almost on top of them,' said Mo.

They raced out of the cockpit. Teejay leaned over the rail, peering at the bank. 'Nothing here. Any your side?'

'Not a sausage,' said Mr Toad. He paused. 'What are we looking for again?'

'Piers,' said Ratty, 'you know, big wooden things that stick out into the water.'

THE
WOOD

'Big wooden things, eh?' Mr Toad cleared his throat. He gazed at the smashed planks around the boat. 'You know, I did hear a bit of a crunching noise.'

'You mean you broke them?' said Ratty.

'Dashed things shouldn't have been there in the first place. A danger to river traffic, if you ask me. Anyhow, it shows we're in the right place,' Mr Toad ran to the ladder and climbed to the ground. 'Come on, chaps. That clue must be here somewhere!'

Teejay, Ratty, and Mo jumped down after him. But the clearing was empty, except for a small sign, that said 'THE WOOD'.

Teejay pulled out the plastic tag. 'The next line says: "You can't see me for the trees." '

'But the trees are miles away,' said Ratty. 'They can't be hiding anything.'

'No, it's a riddle, remember?' said Mo. He ran to the small sign, grabbed it, and started tugging at it. 'See, see? It's "THE WOOD"! That's what it says.'

'Poor chap's gone bananas,' whispered Mr Toad to Teejay. 'Must be the damp.'

Teejay blinked. Then she grinned. 'No, he's a clever Mo. It's a saying, isn't it? "You can't see the wood for the trees." '

'And the sign says "THE WOOD"!' said Ratty. 'So it's the next clue. Nice one, Mo!'

'Stop talking and help me,' panted Mo. Ratty grabbed the sign too, and it came free with a pop. Another tag was hanging from the bottom of it.

'Well done, that Mole!' cried Mr Toad. 'Excellent detective skills in evidence. I believe a song of clue-finding may be appropriate!'

He cleared his throat.

'I wandered lonely as a Toad
Who floats in boats with river views,
When all at once I spied a Mo,
And then Teejay and Ratty too!
With them on board it's quite a breeze,
To solve the clues beneath the trees!'

Mr Toad beamed at them. 'Can you believe I made that up on the spot?'

'Yes,' said Ratty. 'I can.'

'Come on, let's read the next clue!' said Teejay.

Mo opened the tag, and they gathered around . . .

chapter 5

wild wood
and water

Your day is done, the future's to come. Find me tomorrow by the creator's home. I light the way. 51° 28' 59" N 1° 05' 17" W

'Sounds like the next one isn't ready yet,' said Teejay.

'Shame,' said Mr Toad, 'but the article did say that there were only five clues each day.'

'What article?' said Ratty.

Mr Toad pulled a newspaper from his pocket, and gave it to him. 'It's the brand new riverbank periodical,' he said. 'It's called *Wild Wood and Water*. I'd have thought you'd know

41

all about it, being a water rat.'

Ratty shook his head. 'Never heard of it.'

'Well, it's rather exclusive,' said Mr Toad, heading back to his boat. 'They deliver only to the very finest of riverside homes.'

Ratty pulled a face behind his back.

'Speaking of home,' Mr Toad continued, 'it's time we were off. I'll drive!'

Ratty opened the paper. 'Huh. Not much of a newspaper,' he said. 'There's only one page.'

Teejay and Mo read it over his shoulder.

TREASURE-HUNT FEVER GRIPS THE RIVER!

It's the GREAT CLUE HUNT! Prizes to be won!

It's the latest craze! Only BORING people aren't out EVERY DAY solving clues! Hard to believe that some people are still sitting at home when IMPORTANT and INTERESTING people are out ALL DAY solving clues! Get involved!

GREAT PRIZES!

Don't go home! Prove you're the most INTELLIGENT and INTERESTING person around! Solve the clues before everyone else! FIVE NEW CLUES every day! Don't miss out, WIN REALLY GOOD PRIZES!

———

REMEMBER: DON'T GO HOME OR YOU'LL REGRET IT!

'Odd,' Mo frowned.

'Come on, you lot!' shouted Mr Toad. 'Less reading, more action. Now who's for a cream tea at Toad Hall?'

'Yes, please!' shouted Teejay. But then her face fell. 'Oh, we can't. Badge is picking me up from Ratty's house.'

'Ratty's house?' Mr Toad paused, one hand on the ladder. A wistful look crossed his face. 'Yes, I remember. All those reeds and ducks. And the cosy fire, not so far downriver from Toad Hall. I should so like to visit again.' He smiled. 'I know, I'll run you up in my boat. It's on my way home!'

'Great idea!' said Teejay.

'No it isn't,' hissed Ratty.

'Of course it is! Let us depart!' cried Mr Toad. He scrambled up the ladder and into the cockpit. 'All aboard that's coming aboard!'

'Shouldn't we put the clue back?' said Mo.

'And have someone beat us to the prizes?' said Mr Toad. 'Don't be ridiculous. Bring it along.'

Teejay shrugged and began to climb the ladder. But then she caught a movement from across the river. A dark figure in a dinghy

44

paddled out of the shadows under the far trees. For an instant it seemed to stare right at her. And then the dinghy motored away.

Teejay shivered. 'It's like he was watching us or something.'

'I'm not sure I like this clue hunt,' said Mo. 'There's something funny about it.'

The engines roared into life. Mr Toad's boat started to shake.

'Well, *I* don't like Mr Toad's driving,' said Ratty. 'There's nothing funny about that.'

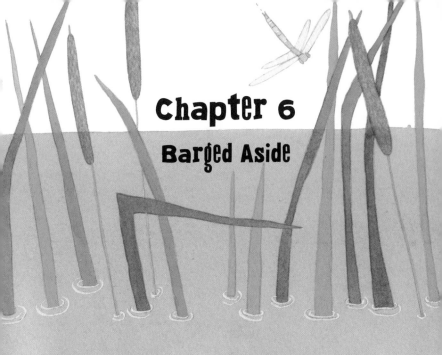

Chapter 6

Barged Aside

Trees blurred by. Teejay held on for dear life as the boat swerved up the river. Ratty's whiskers were flat to his face. Mo clutched the rail, eyes shut.

'Ohhhh!' he moaned. 'Make it stop. I don't feel well.'

'Hehee! Faster, faster!' cried Mr Toad. He turned to Ratty. 'You're a water rat: how do you drive boats faster?'

'Go in a straight line!' yelled Ratty. They shot by a rowing boat, leaving it rocking. 'And you're meant to pass other boats on the left!'

'How am I supposed to know these things?' said Mr Toad.

'I'll teach you!' shouted Ratty.

'Yes, yes, that's it!' cried Mo. 'Let Ratty drive! Please!'

Mr Toad's hands tightened on the wheel. He scowled at the water.

48

'Go on, Mr T,' said Teejay. 'Rat's great with boats. You'll learn loads.'

'Oh, very well.' Mr Toad gave the wheel to Ratty. Then he sat on a locker in a sulk.

Ratty took control and immediately the boat steadied. He steered them smoothly up the river.

'You see?' said Ratty. 'It feels like we're going slower, but we're actually getting there quicker.'

'There's no difference,' said Mr Toad, crossly. 'Except it's not as much fun.'

After a few minutes even Mo let go, and sat next to Teejay on the deck. They lay back and watched the trees and boats drift past.

'Maybe Rat was right about rivers,' said Teejay. 'It's quite nice, really.'

PARP!

Teejay sat up. 'What was that?'

'It wasn't me,' said Mo.

PAAARP!

Teejay got to her feet. 'No. It was those!'

HONK!

Two enormous, rusty barges were heading towards them. Side by side, they honked as they came.

'They're blocking the way,' said Mo. 'What are we going to do?'

'They'll give us room,' said Ratty. 'It's the rules of the river.'

HONK!

PAAARRP! went the barges. **PAAARRRP!**

'I don't think they're going to move,' said Teejay.

'Ha!' Mr Toad leapt to his feet. '**Parp-parp**, is it? Well, if they think they can bully us they've got another think coming.'

He pressed the horn.

Poop-poop!

'Hah! Now they'll move aside.'

PAARRRRP-PAAARRRRP!

'Mr Toad,' said Ratty, 'I think we should—'

'Full speed ahead!' cried Mr Toad. He grabbed the throttle, making the engine roar. 'Don't give way!' He pressed the horn again.

Poop-poop!

PAARRRRP-PAAARRRRP! PAAARRP PAARRP PAAARRRRP!

'There's no space! We'll be squished!' yelled Mo.

'Argh!' shouted Ratty. 'Hold onto something!'

He spun the wheel. Mo tumbled as the deck tilted. Teejay grabbed the rail with one hand, and Mo's foot with the other. The barges honked louder.

PAAARRRPP–PAARRRRP!

They hurtled towards the riverbank. Ratty spun the wheel again. Mo fell against the rail as the deck tilted the other way. He flung his arms over it and clung there.

'Oh, I hate this boat,' Mo whimpered.

And now they were pointing at a tiny gap between the barges and the bank.

'Breathe in, everyone!' called Mr Toad.

Teejay could hear mud and stones scraping beneath the hull. Reeds brushed the sides and low branches snapped overhead.

'Duck!' yelled Teejay.

'This is no time for bird watching,' shouted Mr Toad.

A branch took his hat clean off.

'We're too close,' shouted Ratty. 'Push the barge away!'

Teejay grabbed a pole and shoved it at the nearest barge. She saw a cabin full of dark

53

figures, then black and rusted metal, chains, and stacks of tree trunks. She smelled fumes and saw frothing water. And then the barges were gone, motoring away as if nothing had happened.

Mo sat down on the deck, shaking in relief. Teejay put her pole down. 'Phew! Nice steering, Rat,' she said. 'Not a scratch.'

Mr Toad, though, was leaning over the rail. His jaw fell open. 'What do you mean "not a scratch"? Just look at these ghastly scrapes!'

'*You* did those,' said Ratty.

But Mr Toad had run to the back of the boat. 'You rotten, rampaging river rogues!' he yelled. 'You scurrilous, scurvy scoundrels! Come back and answer for your actions!'

Then Mr Toad came back to the cockpit. 'Well, really!' He shook his head. 'Terrible drivers like that just shouldn't be on the water.'

Chapter 7

The Rats' Riverbank Residence

Teejay spent the rest of the trip watching for barges. But all stayed quiet. And soon they came to a shaded bend, where the water was deep, cool, and green. In the riverbank was a neat hole, with decking on posts jutting over the water. On it Ratty's parents were drinking tea with Ms Badger.

Mr Toad winked at Teejay, and reached for the horn. 'Just a little tinkle to let them know we're here.'

Poop-poop!

'Ack!' Ms Badger jumped, splashing tea over

her clothes.

'Hi, Mum, hi, Dad. Can we moor up?' said Ratty.

'Oh my goodness, hang on!' cried Mrs Rat. She fetched some ropes and threw them to Teejay and Mo. Ratty turned off the engine and made everything shipshape. And then they all jumped down.

'Quite an entrance,' muttered Ms Badger, wiping tea from her skirt. But she smiled at

Teejay. 'At least you're on time for once.'

'Thanks to Mr T,' said Teejay. 'We've been helping with his treasure hunt.'

'That's nice,' said Mrs Rat. 'I hope they haven't been a nuisance, Mr Toad?'

'Very much the contrary, I assure you,' said Mr Toad. 'They're my crack clue-solving squad. And Ratty is a fine sailor. The way he dodged those barges was worthy of Toad himself!'

'*Dodged those barges?*' cried Ms Badger. 'What do you mean "dodged those barges"?'

'I tell you what,' said Mr Rat, quickly.

'How about some nice tea and scones?'

Mr Toad rubbed his hands together. 'Capital idea! And might there perhaps be a smidgeon of jam or a spoonful of cream?'

'Of course. I'll bring some plates.' Mr Rat disappeared into the house.

Ms Badger frowned at Teejay, Ratty, and Mo. 'Explain.'

'It wasn't our fault, Badge,' said Teejay. 'They blocked the river. Ratty did really well.'

'Without his skill we'd have been crushed,' declared Mr Toad. 'Smashed to smithereens! Bludgeoned to bite-sized bits of boat!'

Ms Badger raised her paws to her forehead.

'Those dratted barges,' said Mrs Rat. 'They've been going up and down all week.'

'But where are they coming from?' said Teejay.

Mrs Rat gazed at Mr Toad. 'Nobody knows. But some say they're loading up at Toad Hall.'

'Toad Hall? My dear lady that's quite impossible,' said Mr Toad. 'I think I'd know if

someone was using my new dock. After all, I need it for my boat!'

Mr Rat came out carrying a tray. 'You know, there's been a lot of odd talk, and not only about barges.' He passed the scones around. 'The ducks say they keep seeing dinghies everywhere.'

'Dinghies,' hissed Mo to Teejay, 'like the one we saw!'

'We should talk to Otter,' Mr Rat continued. 'He knows everything that's happening on the river.'

Mr Toad looked alarmed. 'You don't think this could interrupt my treasure hunt? I'm sure I'm in the lead by now! And I'll need my clue-squad out tomorrow if I'm to stay there.'

'Ooh, can we, Badge?' said Teejay. 'We'll be really careful!'

'Not a chance,' said Ms Badger. 'It's school, remember?'

'School? Who needs school?' cried Mr Toad. 'There's no finer education than boating with the ingenious Toad!'

Ms Badger folded her arms. 'They're not missing

school. But if Mr and Mrs Rat agree then maybe they can visit you on Saturday.' She frowned at Mr Toad. 'But *only* if they promise not to set foot on your boat.'

'My dear lady—' protested Mr Toad.

'We promise, we promise,' said Mo, quickly.

'But—' said Teejay.

'Deal!' said Ms Badger. 'And I mean it, Teejay: no going on his boat. You'll have to find another way to help.'

Teejay sighed. 'Yes, Badge.'

'Very well,' Mr Toad sighed. 'I shall pursue my endeavour unaided: a lone captain of my noble vessel.' He gazed at his boat. 'I say, I don't suppose anyone on the river might have mentioned my new boat?'

'Oh yes,' said Mrs Rat. '*Everyone's* talking about it.'

'Well, that's marvellous,' said Mr Toad, looking pleased. 'I do like to make a splash!'

Mr Rat poured him a cup of tea. 'Yes. That's what everyone said.'

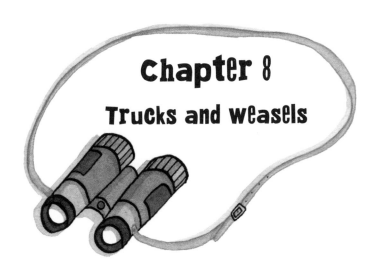

Chapter 8

Trucks and weasels

'That was the longest week ever,' said Teejay, cycling towards Toad Hall's gates. 'I don't even know if Mr Toad's still solving clues.'

'Don't worry, he is,' called Ratty behind her. 'Dad says he's been annoying everyone all week. Otter's going to have words with him.'

'That doesn't sound too bad,' said Mo.

'You haven't met Otter,' said Ratty. 'He's scary.'

'Ooh, here are the gates,' said Teejay. 'Remember, it's a race to the front door. Ready, steady—'

'Argh! Dodge!' yelled Mo.

Teejay swerved as a truck thundered past. It raced out of the gates and away up the road. She skidded to a stop. 'What's going on?'

A queue of trucks went past the front door and around the back of Toad Hall.

'Is Mr Toad collecting lorries now?' said Mo.

'Not unless he's collecting weasels too,' said Ratty. 'Look over there!'

A group of stoats and weasels in overalls were standing under a tree, chatting and drinking tea from flasks.

'Trucks and weasels,' said Teejay. 'That's a recipe for trouble. Come on!'

They hid their bikes and ran into Toad Hall's grounds. Teejay, Ratty, and Mo dashed

from tree to tree, following the queue to the back of the house. They dived into a bush, out of sight.

'Ouch!' said Mo. 'It's spiky.'

'Shh!' Teejay hissed. 'What's happening, Rat?'

Ratty pulled binoculars from his pocket. 'Weirdness is happening, that's what. It's a mess.' He handed the binoculars to Teejay. 'They're using Mr Toad's new dock.'

Where there had once been a bank of reeds and sedges, was an enormous concrete platform. Lorries carrying tree trunks were beeping and reversing up to it. Weasels dashed about, pulling on ropes and dumping the trunks into barges.

'But Mr Toad said he didn't know about the barges,' said Mo. 'How could he miss all this?'

'No idea. But I know how to find out,' said Teejay. 'This way.'

She led them down through the bushes to the reeds at the water's edge. Just beyond, in the river, floated a shiny white boat.

WEASELY ENDEAVOUR

'It's called the *Weasely Endeavour*,' hissed Ratty.

'And the Chief Weasel's on it,' said Mo. 'Look!'

A large weasel in a suit and a life jacket leaned on the boat's rail. 'More of our trees off to the sawmill, Mr Ripton,' he said. 'Such a pleasure to see Toad Hall being put to a profitable use. Especially Wildwood Industrious's profit. **Hurk hurk**.'

The tall grey weasel next to him smiled.

'We could build our own, but think of the cost,' the Chief Weasel continued. Mr Ripton whispered in his ear. 'And you're right, of course, Mr Ripton. It is best if people don't know we're cutting down trees. They get so upset about these things.'

Mr Ripton cleared his throat, and tapped his watch.

'Quite right, we shouldn't overstay our welcome.' The Chief Weasel clicked his fingers at a weasel on the dock, who spoke

71

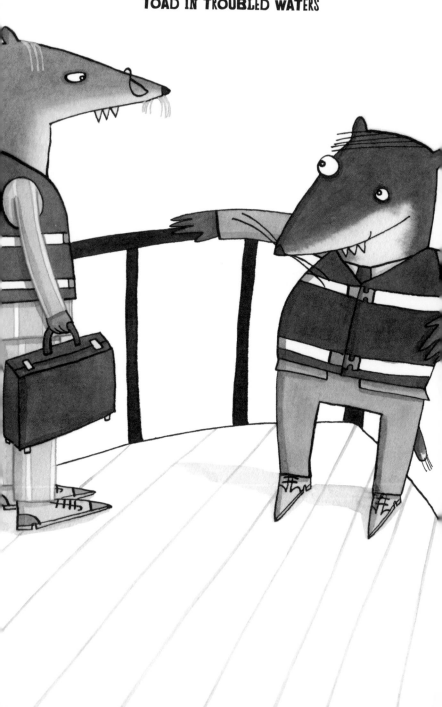

quickly into a walkie-talkie.

'Dinghy Two, Dinghy Two, this is Wilbur at *Weasely Endeavour*. What's your Toad status, Wesley?' Wilbur listened, then shouted up to the boat: 'Wesley says that Toady hasn't made it to the bridge yet. He's stuck on today's second clue.'

'Excellent!' The Chief Weasel rubbed his hands together. 'We have all afternoon. Should we make tomorrow's clues simpler, Mr Ripton? We wouldn't want poor Mr Toad out all night. He needs all the beauty sleep he can get. Hurk hurk.'

'Ooh,' Teejay whispered, '*he* can talk.'

'Hang on,' said Mo, 'that means Wildwood Industrious set the treasure hunt.'

Teejay nodded. 'But why?'

'To keep Mr Toad busy,' said Ratty. 'So they can use his dock.'

'Right.' Teejay's jaw set. 'We've got to find Mr Toad and tell him.'

'But he could be anywhere *down* the river,'

said Mo.

'Then we need a boat.'

'Um, you promised Ms Badger, remember?' said Ratty.

Teejay grinned. 'I promised not to go on *Mr Toad's* boat. I didn't say anything about other people's.'

'Oh *no*,' Mo groaned. 'I have a bad feeling about this.'

Chapter 9
That sinking feeling

'**H**uh. Don't know what I was worried about,' said Mo. 'We'll never find anything at this rate.'

Teejay glared at him. She was rowing with one oar while Ratty pulled the other. It felt as though they had been going for hours.

'If you want to go faster, you row,' Ratty puffed.

'I'm on lookout,' said Mo, 'because you're both facing the wrong way. Anyway won't your mum and dad notice their boat's gone?'

'I hope not,' said Ratty. 'I'm not allowed to use it.'

'Tell them it's an emergency,' said Teejay.

'If Mum finds out, it will be an emergency,' said Ratty.

Chugga-Chugga-Chugga-Chugga-Chugga.

'Can you hear something?' said Teejay.

'What's up ahead, Mo?' said Ratty. 'I can't see.'

'Hang on, my glasses are steamed up.' Mo took them off and cleaned them on his T-shirt. 'Oh, now they're smeary.'

Chugga-Chugga-Chugga-Chugga.

'Mo, it's getting louder!' said Teejay.

'Wait a second.' Mo rubbed his glasses again.

CHUGGA-CHUGGA-CHUGGA-CHUGGA.

'Mo, what's going on?' Ratty shouted.

Mo put on his glasses. He froze. Then he yelled, 'Barges! Row for the bank, row for the bank!'

Ratty yanked on his oar, spinning the boat around. 'Pull!' he shouted to Teejay. 'Pull!'

CHUGGA-CHUGGA-CHUGGA-CHUGGA.

Teejay pulled as hard as she could. Their boat surged towards the riverbank.

'Faster, faster,' cried Mo. 'You've got to go—'

WRRORRRWWRRRRTTRRROOOOWWMMM!

A barge went right past the back of their boat.

'Phew,' said Teejay. 'That was close. I thought we were going to—'

Clank!

A chain smashed into them, spinning their boat in the water.

'Whoa!' Teejay clutched her seat. Mo tumbled to the floor. Ratty dropped his oar.

Chugga-Chugga-Chugga-Chugga . . .

The sound of the barges faded.

'Amazing: we're OK!' said Teejay. She paused. 'Um, why are my feet wet?'

Ratty pointed to the back of the boat. 'Because we're not OK.'

The chain had split the wood. And now water was pouring in.

'We're sinking, we're sinking!' shouted Mo.

'I can see that,' Ratty yelled. 'Paddle for the bank!'

'Start emptying, Mo!' Teejay grabbed her oar and rowed as hard as she could. Mo scooped water, tipping it over the side. But it was coming in too quickly.

'The boat's . . . getting . . . heavy,' gasped Ratty.

'And slow!' Teejay panted. 'And the bank's miles away.'

'We're not going to make it,' cried Mo. 'We're going to sink. Oh, what happens if we sink?'

'What do you *think* happens?' Ratty snapped.

'We get wet!' said Teejay.

'And then my parents kill me. Keep going!' cried Ratty.

But it was no good. The water rose to Teejay's knees. She swallowed. 'Does anyone have a really, really good plan for getting out of this?'

Ratty and Mo shook their heads.

'No,' said Teejay. 'Me neither.'

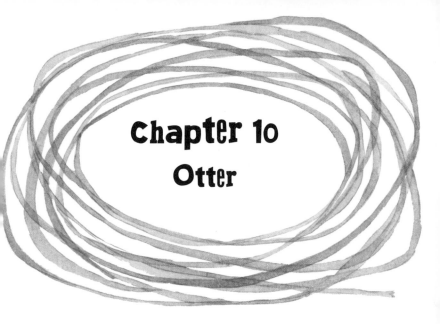

Chapter 10
Otter

A rope flew through the air. It landed with a splash beside Teejay.

'Quick, you lot,' shouted a voice. 'Take hold of it!'

Teejay snatched the rope and threw the free end to Ratty and Mo.

'Now pull!' yelled the voice. 'Pull as hard as you can.'

'Come on,' said Teejay. 'All together, heave!'

They hauled on the rope. The boat tipped dangerously. More water poured in. But they began to move across the river.

'That's it, we're doing it!' said Teejay.
'We're moving! Heave!'

The boat rocked and sank lower. But
they were going faster and faster. They
pulled again, and again, then *clunk!* They
struck the side of something metal.

'It's a barge! We've crashed!' Mo
ducked, paws over his head.

'No, it's my narrowboat,' said the voice,
right above them. 'Aboard, aboard, quickly
now.' A huge, webbed paw reached down.

Ratty took it, and was hoisted from the boat. The paw reappeared.

'Go on, Mo, take hold,' said Teejay.

But Mo did not move. The paw grabbed him by his collar. 'Ouf!' said Mo, as he was yanked from view. His feet disappeared up over the side. And then the paw was back.

'Young Ms Toad, if you'd be so kind?'

Teejay clutched the paw with both hands.

'Whee!' Teejay was lifted into the air. Then her feet thudded onto the deck of a canal boat. Next to her, Ratty and Mo were standing in a puddle.

'That was fun! Thank you!' Teejay looked around for the boat's owner. But he had disappeared over the rail.

'Where did he go?' she hissed to Ratty.

'It's Otter,' Ratty whispered. 'He's like that.'

Otter shouted up from the water, 'Your boat's done for, lad. A crying shame; she looked like a good 'un. Coil that rope by the cleat there. I'll be back up.'

Otter's grey-whiskered face popped up over the side. He threw up two oars, and stomped onto the deck.

'They're all I could save.'

Teejay, Ratty, and Mo watched bubbles rise from Ratty's boat. Then it sank to the bottom of the river.

'Oh,' said Mo. 'That's quite sad, really.'

'Well, you're not hurt, so it's all right,' said Otter. 'But it was foolish to get stuck like that.' He frowned at Ratty. 'I'd expect a mole and a

toad to have trouble on the
water, but you should have
known better.'

Ratty hung his head.

'But it wasn't Rat's fault,' said Teejay. 'That
barge put a hole in our boat.'

'Ack, barges.' Otter glared out at the river.
'It would be. I'm sick to death of 'em scaring
all the fish away. If it's not them then it's that
buffoon of a Toad in his overpriced bath-toy.'

'But—' said Teejay.

'Oh, I've nothing against Mr Toad; everyone knows that,' said Otter. 'But it's high time he learned the ways of the river. Gallivanting around, letting weasels create mayhem with their logs and dinghies. It's not good enough!'

'You know about the weasels?' said Teejay.

'I know all about them. And I'll fettle 'em and no mistake. But first I want a word with Toad. Why did he give them Toad Hall's dock, eh? What did he think he was doing?'

'He doesn't know, Mr Otter,' said Mo. 'They invented a game to keep him away so they could use his dock without him knowing.'

'A game, is it? That treasure hunt I've been hearing of, no doubt.' Otter scratched his whiskers. 'A bad business, this. Wild Wooders at Toad Hall, filling the river with dead trees. Not a moment's peace or a fish to be had, and all because they've got Toad in one of his fads.' He folded his arms. 'There's only one thing to be done: we shall find Toad and make him see sense.'

Chapter 11
Hoodwinked

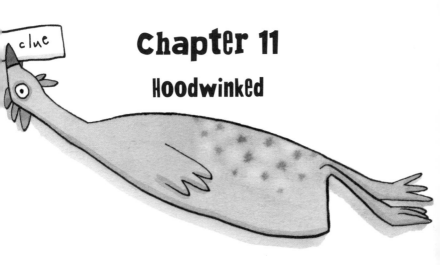

'**B**oat ahoy!' yelled Ratty. He grinned at Teejay. 'I've always wanted to say that.'

Teejay shaded her eyes with her hands. Then she spotted Mr Toad's boat, bobbing at the riverbank. It was even more battered than before.

Otter motored them alongside. 'Toad! Are you aboard, there?'

'Go away!' came Mr Toad's voice. 'I'm terribly busy, can't you see?'

Otter's brows lowered. 'Toad, it's Otter. Get out here immediately.'

Mr Toad flung open the cabin. 'Otter, my dear fellow, why didn't you say so? Come aboard, come aboard. This really is the most wonderful coincidence!'

'Coincidence?' growled Otter, stepping over the rail. 'What coincidence?'

'Well, here was I thinking to myself, Toady,

Little Po

old chap, it's your last clue of the day, and you're stumped,' said Mr Toad. 'What you need is help from a real expert in rivers and boats and what-have-you. And here you are!'

Otter frowned. 'Now, see here—' he began.

'Let me show you!' cried Mr Toad. He grabbed a rubber chicken and waved it under Otter's nose.

'Ha ha! Look, it's a chicken!' Then Mr Toad lowered his voice to a hiss. 'It's not a chicken. It's a clue. But shh! Tell nobody. There could be spies.'

'Um, I don't think Mr Otter's interested in your chicken,' said Teejay.

'Only because he's a good-hearted and honest fellow!' cried Mr Toad. 'And that's why I can trust him, d'you see? You must help me solve my clues!'

'I'll help you, all right,' said Otter. He held a finger under Mr Toad's nose. 'I'll help you see you're being hoodwinked by weasels.'

'Hoodwinked by weasels? What nonsense

is this?' cried Mr Toad. 'The cunning Toad has never been hoodwinked, least of all by weasels!'

'But Mr T, there are weasels—' Teejay began.

'Weasels? Where?' Mr Toad held his telescope to his eye. 'I see no weasels.'

'Take your boat back to Toad Hall,' said Otter. 'You'll find plenty there.'

'Abandon my quest while I'm winning? You must be joking. All my precious clues would be snapped up in an instant.'

Mr Toad folded his arms. 'No, no, you're quite wrong, I'm sure of it.'

'You're being ridiculous,' Otter growled.

'An insult!' cried Mr Toad. 'I thought you came to help, but now I see you're intent on scoffing! Otter, you should leave. My quest is everything. I'll go where my clues tell me and nowhere else! And that's my final word.'

And Mr Toad put his hands over his ears.

'Great. Now what do we do?' Teejay hissed.

'Otter's right: we have to get him to Toad Hall,' said Mo. 'It's the only way he'll see.'

'But how? Mr Toad won't go anywhere unless it's written on a clue,' said Ratty.

Mo blinked. 'Of course! We'll solve his clue. That's exactly what we'll do.'

'*What?*' said Ratty. 'How's that going to help?'

'Trust me,' said Mo. 'I've got a plan. We have to solve that clue!'

Chapter 12
The
Loudest Bark?

Otter scowled at Mr Toad. 'You can refuse to listen, you selfish animal, but don't come crying when you fall foul of the Wild Wooders.' He turned to Teejay. 'Come on, we'll leave Toad to his folly.'

Teejay grabbed Otter's arm. 'Change of plan. We have to help him with the clue.'

Ratty and Mo nodded. Otter stared. He threw up his paws. 'Everyone on this boat is quite, quite mad. Very well, Mr Toad, we shall help you.' He gave Teejay a stern look. 'But there had better be a good reason for this.'

Mr Toad took his hands from his ears. 'You mean it? You'll really help old Toady? Oh, my dear sir, thank you, thank you!' He danced a small jig for joy. Then he pulled the tag from the rubber chicken. 'Here's the troublesome fellow!'

They gathered around.

Find the noisiest bark, where the fish keep their money. I can do the splits. 51° 33' 48" N 0° 44' 55" W

'That's stupid,' said Ratty. 'Fish don't have money.'

'It's fiendish. I don't even know where to start looking,' said Mr Toad.

'Start on the bank,' Mo grinned. 'Because that's where fish keep their money!'

'What?' Teejay blinked. 'Oh, a riverbank, I get it.'

'Ha!' Otter gave Mo a hearty clap on the shoulder. 'Well done, lad.'

'A stunning deduction!' cried Mr Toad. 'But what about this noisy bark? I haven't seen a dog all day.'

'It's boats, I reckon, not dogs,' said Otter, slowly. '"Bark" is an old word for boat.' He smiled. 'It's what my dad used to call them.'

'Why, then it's simplicity itself!' shouted Mr Toad. He leapt down to the bank and ran to where dozens of small boats were pulled up on the grass. He ripped the cover off the nearest and dived inside.

Clang! Bang! Crash!

Rowlocks, life jackets, planks, nets, and oars thudded onto the grass as Mr Toad hurled them into a heap. He climbed out and stared at the pile. 'Can any of these things do the splits?'

'I don't think so,' said Ratty.

'Drat. Stupid things.' Mr Toad thumped the empty boat.

Thump!

'Ooh, ooh,' cried Teejay. 'Hit a different one, Mr T!'

'If you say so.'

Thunk!

'See, it's a different noise. Do another!' said Teejay.

'Young lady,' said Otter, severely, 'why are you encouraging this reprobate of a Toad to thump people's boats?'

'Because we want the noisiest bark,' said

Teejay. 'Get it?'

'Oh, *I* do!' said Mo. 'Noisiest boat. The ones with less in them will sound louder.'

'Exactly: I think the clue's in an empty boat,' said Teejay.

'Brilliant,' cried Mr Toad. 'We need a consignment of hull-thumpers down here, pronto!'

They jumped down to the bank, even Otter. And soon the air was ringing with *thumps* and *thunks*.

'Ha ha! Thump!' shouted Mr Toad. 'Thumpitty, thumpitty, thump!'

Boom!

Everyone stopped. The noise came from the boat in front of Otter. He rapped it again with his knuckles.

Boom! Boom!

'That's the fellow!' said Mr Toad. 'That's the very fellow! Quickly now!'

They lifted the cover from the boat. Inside was a single banana. Mr Toad grabbed it. 'It does the splits! Ha ha! A banana split,' he chucked. 'Clever Toady, I solved it again!'

The first clue of tomorrow,
I spy. Find me where the
weasels lie. You might be
stumped and so might I!
51° 34' 12" N 1° 16' 14" W

Chapter 13
Pernicious Treachery

Mr Toad pulled the tag from the banana.

The first clue of tomorrow, I spy. Find me where the weasels lie. You might be stumped and so might I! 51° 34' 12" N 1° 14' 14" W

'That's it,' hissed Mo. 'That's what we need. Quick, Rat, get a photo!'

Ratty pulled out a camera. Mo stared at it. 'That's *ancient*.'

'I know! Good, isn't it?' Ratty pressed the button. The camera whirred and a white photograph came out.

'What's that you have?' demanded Mr Toad.

His mouth dropped open as the image of the clue became clearer. 'You took a photograph? But why would you—' He broke off with a gasp. 'Oh! Oh, perfidy! So *that's* why you wanted me to abandon my quest!'

'Sorry, what?' said Teejay.

'You wanted me gone, so you could solve the clues in my place!' Mr Toad stared all about him. 'Then you'll all be free to claim the prizes with this Otter fellow!'

'Toad, you're a fool,' snapped Otter.

'You're right, I was a fool!' cried Mr Toad. 'I was a fool to trust you, or to count you as my friends.' He burst out sobbing. 'Treachery, oh, pernicious and unkind treachery!'

Teejay stared at him in horror. 'Mr T, we're not—'

'No more words!' shouted Mr Toad. 'I've heard enough deceitfulness!' He dashed his tears away. 'I'll win the hunt without you, you'll see! There's nobody here solves clues like me!'

PERNICIOUS TREACHERY

TOAD IN TROUBLED WATERS

I am a Toad on a quest for a prize,
Surrounded by tricks and deception and lies!
I thought we were friends, but you're set on
betrayal,
But with or without you the Toad shall
prevail!'

Then Mr Toad ran to his boat.
Before anyone could move he
had scuttled up the ladder
and started the engines.

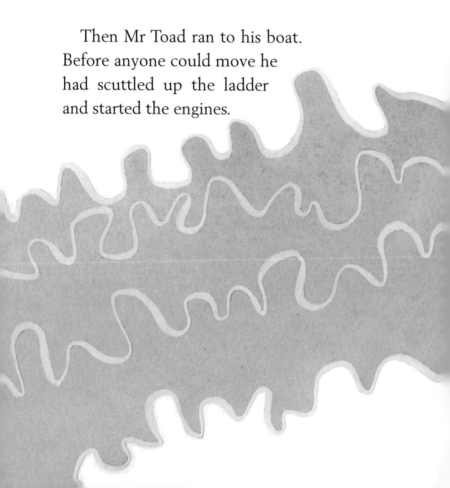

He roared off upriver, back towards Toad Hall.

Ratty watched him go. 'That went well.'

'Oh, poor Mr T,' said Teejay. 'He thinks we betrayed him!'

'Poor Mr Toad nothing,' growled Otter. 'He's a first-class idiot who doesn't deserve his friends.' He folded his arms.

'Now would anyone care to explain exactly what we're meant to have achieved?'

'Mr Toad didn't want to go to Toad Hall,' said Mo. 'But now we can tell him to go there.

We can tell him with clues!'

Ratty looked at Teejay. 'Any idea what he's talking about?'

'It's simple! We just have to swap the next clue for one that sends him on a different treasure hunt. One that *we've* written,' Mo grinned. 'One that ends at Toad Hall!'

'Right when the weasels think he's gone,' said Teejay. 'Clever Mo! He'll catch them red-pawed!'

'And, thanks to this photograph, we know where the next clue is,' said Otter. 'Bravo, Mole. I should never have doubted you.'

Ratty, though, was frowning. 'What about the dinghies? There are weasels watching everything. If we mess with a clue, they'll just tell the Chief.'

'Oh. And then they'll pack up and leave,' said Teejay.

The grin left Mo's face. 'Oh dear. I hadn't thought of that.'

Otter banged the tiller with his paw. 'If the dinghy-weasels are a nuisance then we'll just have to deal with them.'

'How?' said Ratty.

'I'm calling a state of river emergency.' Otter smiled, fiercely. 'And do you know what water folk do in an emergency?'

Teejay looked at Ratty and Mo. They shook their heads.

'I'll tell you.' Otter rubbed his paws together. 'We do *pirating!*'

Chapter 14
Plundering Pirates!

oh argh!

'I feel ridiculous,' said Ms Badger. 'I don't know how you talked me into this.'

'You look great,' said Teejay. 'The stripes go with your fur.' Ms Badger looked fearsome in a striped jumper, a headscarf, and an eyepatch. 'You too, Mr Rat.'

Mr Rat stared at the toy sword he was holding. 'I'm not sure I'm cut out for pirating. I think I'm too polite.'

'Keep it quiet!' ordered Otter. 'They'll hear us.'

'Sorry,' whispered Teejay. She stared out

at the pre-dawn shadows. 'I wish the weasels would hurry up. It's spooky here.'

They were aboard Otter's narrowboat, hidden beneath the Wild Wood trees.

'It's just the wood at night,' whispered Ms Badger. 'I used to visit Grandpa badger here when I was a cub. Besides, we're the pirates, remember!'

'Good point!' Teejay grinned.

'Shh! Here comes our dinghy-weasel!' hissed Otter. 'Action stations, everyone!'

B r r r r r o o w w b r r r r r o o w - brrrrrowbrrrrroww-brrrrrrbrrrrr!

A weasel in a dinghy motored to a stop at the far bank. He got out and ran into the gloom.

'He's setting the clue,' whispered Teejay, 'right where Mo said he would.'

The weasel lifted a tree stump, dropped something under it, and slipped back into his dinghy. Then he set off, paddling across the river towards where they were hiding.

'That's it!' hissed Otter. 'Pirate time!' He threw a switch. Floodlights shone out, lighting a black pirate flag. The narrowboat roared into life. 'Signal the bank team! Prepare to board the weasel.' He raised his voice and yelled, 'Haaarrg!'

'Aaarrr!' yelled Ms Badger.

'Shiver me timbers! Splice the mainbrace! Aaarr!' shouted Teejay.

'Er, hello there!' cried Mr Rat.

Otter raced them towards the dinghy. 'Who

are you?' squeaked the weasel. 'W-what do you want?'

'Does ye want to know?' shouted Otter. 'Does ye *really* want to know?'

The weasel hesitated. 'No, not really. Can you go away, please?'

'Go away?' roared Otter. 'We be pirates! We don't be going nowhere without plunder!'

'I-I don't have any plunder,' the weasel quavered. On the bank behind him Teejay saw Ratty, Mo, and Mrs Rat dash to where the clue was hidden.

'Aaar!' yelled Ms Badger. 'No plunder, ye say? You wouldn't be tricksy, would ye? Not if ye doesn't wish to be walkin' the plank!'

'Or get a taste o' the cutlass!' shouted Otter.

'Oh, please,' squeaked the weasel, 'I don't think I like cutlass.'

On the far bank, Ratty ran back to the water's edge. He gave Teejay the thumbs up. Then he, Mrs Rat, and Mo rushed away towards their hidden boat.

'They're done!' Teejay whispered to Otter.

Otter nodded and glared at the weasel. 'What be your name, scurvy dog? Be ye not

Weaselbeard the Feared?'

'W-who?'

'Weaselbeard the Feared. The mangiest son of a stoat e'er to sail the seven seas.'

'N-no. I'm W-Wesley. Wesley the frightened.'

'Curse the pirate gods!' cried Otter. 'He not be Weaselbeard. Call off the boarding, lads!'

'And lasses,' hissed Ms Badger.

Wesley sagged with relief. 'You mean . . . I can go?'

'That ye can!' said Otter. 'We seek only Weaselbeard!'

'Terribly sorry for the inconvenience,' said Mr Rat.

Ms Badger elbowed him in the ribs. But Wesley hadn't noticed.

'Oh, thank you!' cried Wesley. 'Thank you, thank you!'

'Haaarr!' cried Otter one last time. Then he steered the narrowboat off and away up the river.

'I think it worked,' said Teejay. 'He didn't

see Mo switch the clues. Oh, look, and here comes Mr Toad!'

They ducked behind the railing as Mr Toad's boat raced past. But Mr Toad did not even look up from his satnav.

'Well done, pirates!' said Otter, when he was gone. 'The clue is swapped and Toad is on his way to find it. We'll win the day yet!'

'Pirating is *fun!*' said Ms Badger. 'Did you enjoy it, Mr Rat?'

'Not really. I forgot to ask for any doubloons,' said Mr Rat, sadly.

'Well, you'll get plenty more chances,' said Otter, rubbing his paws together. 'Because once we've dropped off Teejay we'll have a busy day's pirating ahead.'

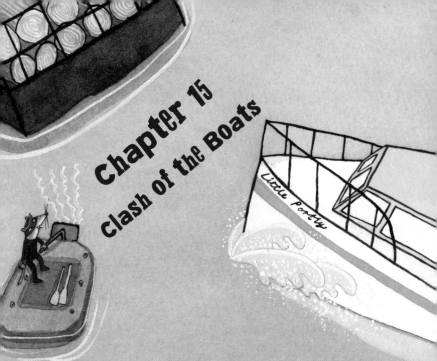

Chapter 15
Clash of the Boats

Teejay, Ratty, and Mo ran up the channel to Toad Hall's boathouse. They slipped quietly over the bridge, past the lorries, and then scuttled down behind the reeds at Toad Hall's dock.

'Phew, made it,' Mo whispered. 'Now we just wait for Mr Toad.'

'I hope the weasels don't go before he gets here,' hissed Ratty.

Teejay peeked out through the reeds. 'I think it's OK. They're still loading trees.'

But a panicking weasel raced past their

117

hiding spot. He skidded to a stop at the *Weasely Endeavour*.

'Sir, sir, trouble with the dinghies!' panted the weasel. 'They say there's pirates, looking for weasels with beards!'

The Chief Weasel scowled down from the deck of his boat. 'Wilbur, you're blithering nonsense.'

'But it's true, sir,' Wilbur cried. 'There's pirates with hooks and swords and shouting *"Aarr"* and everything!'

'Pirates? On a river? Don't be ridiculous,' snarled the Chief Weasel. 'Tell the dinghies to get back to work. I want to know where that Toad is!'

Wilbur spoke quickly into his walkie-talkie. 'He's gone! He isn't by any of the clues.'

Mr Ripton bent to whisper in the Chief Weasel's ear. The Chief Weasel stared at him. 'We're not packing up, Mr Ripton, dearie me, no. We'd lose a whole day's profit!' The Chief Weasel shook his head. 'There's no cause for concern. Toady's lost, that's all—we made the clues too hard for his tiny brain. **Hurk hurk**. Our plan is foolproof!'

'Hah,' muttered Mo. 'That's what he thinks. We'll sink his plan!'

'You don't think we *did* make the last clue too hard?' whispered Teejay.

'No way,' said Mo. 'Look, here's a copy of the clue we left.' He held out a piece of paper that said:

The hunt is done, you've nearly won. Get here soon—run, run run. We're waiting at Toad Hall with your prize. 51° 29' 03" N 1° 02' 13" W

'Even Mr T can solve that,' said Teejay. 'Good work. He'll come here, and then he can't miss the weasels!'

Ratty, though, frowned at the tag. 'Um, Mo. Those co-ordinates . . . where do they point to?'

Mo grinned. 'Bang in the middle of Mr Toad's dock.'

'Right. So I think we may have a teeny-weeny little problem.'

'What problem?' said Teejay.

RRRRuuM-vRRuuMMM-BRRuRRR-vRRRuMMM . . .

Ratty pointed down the river. Mr Toad's boat swerved around the bend. It was a long way away, but coming fast.

'You know how Mr Toad doesn't look out of the window when he's driving?' said Ratty.

'Oh yes, he just follows the satnav, doesn't he?' said Mo. He blinked. 'But that means—'

'It means he's going to hit the barges,' finished Teejay. She stared at Ratty and Mo. 'Oh no! Run for it!'

. . . RRRRUUM-VRRUUMMM-BRRURRR-VRRRUMMM . . .

Teejay sprinted away from the river, with Ratty and Mo right behind. All around them weasels stopped and stared.

'Run!' Teejay shouted at them. 'Run, run!'

. . . RRRRUUM-VRRUUMMM-BRRURRR-VRRRUMMM . . .

Then the weasels saw Mr Toad's boat. They panicked, dashing away from the water.

Mo glanced over his shoulder. 'Oh no, oh no, oh no, he's going too fast.'

. . . RRRRUUM-VRRUUMMM-BRRURRR-VRRRUMMM . . .

'Way too fast!' shouted Ratty. 'He's going to—'

BANG! Crump! Screech!

Mr Toad's boat smacked into the first barge

123

and ricocheted away. The barge spun, knocking into the other. Trees toppled, rolling into the water.

And Mr Toad drove straight into the side of the Chief Weasel's boat.

Smash! Thump! Bang! Tinkle!

Everyone stopped moving. All eyes were on the boats.

Glug.

'I can't look. What happened?' Mo's face was in his paws.

Glug! Glug!

Bubbles rose and popped as both boats began to fill with water.

'Well, you know how you said we'd sink the weasels?' said Ratty to Mo.

Mo nodded.

'I think we just did.'

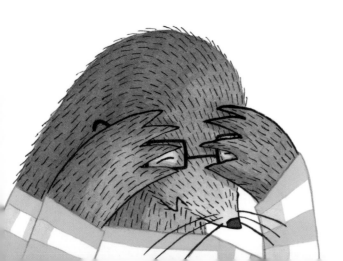

Chapter 16

The Great Detective

Mr Toad sprang onto the deck of his boat. He leapt to the dock. Not even glancing at the chaos he had caused, he sprinted straight up towards the children.

'I did it, I did it!' he cried. He held up a cuddly toy weasel. 'I've solved the last and final clue! I've won, I tell you. I'm the greatest detective who ever lived!' He stopped and frowned at Teejay. 'Well, I was expecting a better reception. Where are the dignitaries? Where are the prizes?'

'Are you OK, Mr T?' said Teejay.

'Of course! I'm magnificent! I've won, don't you see?'

'But what about the accident?' said Ratty.

'This was no accident! I won on purpose, because I'm the best and most incredible Toad! Now there should be prizes! It says it here.'

He waved his copy of *Wild Wood and Water*.

'There aren't any prizes,' said Mo.

'My dear young Mole, have you gone stark raving mad?'

'But Mo's right,' said Teejay. 'That's what we've been trying to tell you.'

'It was weasels all along,' said Ratty. 'They made up the treasure hunt to keep you away

from Toad Hall.'

'So they could use your dock to load up timber,' said Mo.

'Weasels? Here at Toad Hall?' scoffed Mr Toad. 'Balderdash! Pish and nonsense! Do you honestly think I wouldn't have spotted weasels at my home? I'm an expert detective! I'd have seen clues and traces of their presence.' He hesitated. 'Why are you all looking at me like that?'

Teejay put her hands on Mr Toad's shoulders. She turned him to face the river. His jaw dropped open.

Lorries were reversing and fleeing for the gates. Weasels and stoats were running about, or climbing from the river, dripping wet. Mr Toad's boat had sunk, lying on its side. Only the very top of the *Weasely Endeavour* was above the water.

'B-b-but those are weasels,' said Mr Toad, 'and they're at Toad Hall.'

'Yep,' said Ratty, 'he's an expert detective.'

Mr Toad stared at the cuddly weasel in his hands. 'No treasure hunt,' he mumbled. 'No prizes. Just a dockful of weasels.' He closed his eyes. 'Oh, and you tried to tell me. You even came to find me.' Tears began to stream down his cheeks. 'And how did Toad repay your loyalty? By accusing you of betrayal. Oh, what a blind and selfish animal I've been.' He hung his head.

'It's fine, Mr T,' said Teejay. 'It's just like last time.'

'We're used to it,' Mo added.

Mr Toad blinked at them. 'Really?'

Ratty grinned. 'You do this sort of thing quite a lot.'

Mr Toad wiped his eyes. A sheepish smile spread over his face. 'I suppose I do get a bit carried away on occasion.' Then he sighed. 'But Otter was right. I am a silly old fool.'

'Well, never mind,' said Teejay. 'What are you going to do about the weasels?'

She pointed to the soggy weasels milling around by the river.

Mr Toad's eyes narrowed. 'Hmm. Weasels,' he said. He raised his chin. 'I believe it's high time I had a word with those weasels.'

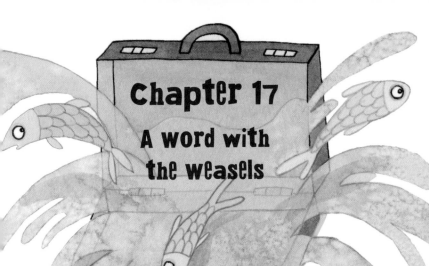

Chapter 17

A word with the weasels

Mr Toad marched down to the dock. The Chief Weasel was being helped from the river by two stoats. Behind him Mr Ripton was emptying water from his briefcase.

'I say,' called Mr Toad, cheerily, 'is everyone all right?'

'No thanks to you, Toady,' snarled the Chief Weasel. 'Look what you've done!'

'Yes, it is rather a mess,' said Mr Toad. 'And you don't seem very pleased to see me.'

'Pleased?' The Chief Weasel goggled at him. 'Why should I be pleased?'

'Because I've won your treasure hunt.'
Mr Toad held up his copy of *Wild Wood and
Water*.

The Chief Weasel scowled at it. Mr Ripton
whispered urgently in his ear.

'That's right, Mr Ripton,' said the Chief
Weasel. 'We don't know anything about a
treasure hunt.'

'But I thought that was why you were here:
to celebrate my victory!' Mr Toad gave the
Chief Weasel an innocent smile.
'Because otherwise you'd
be trespassing at Toad
Hall. And that would
be illegal, wouldn't
it?'

Mr Ripton whispered again. The Chief Weasel glared at him. Then he clenched his paws and rasped, 'Congratulations on winning the *Wild Wood and Water* treasure hunt, Mr Toad. How clever of you.'

'There you go,' said Mr Toad, cheerfully. 'I knew that's why you were here. Oh, look, here come my friends.'

Otter's narrowboat chugged down towards the dock, steering carefully through the tree trunks and sunken boats.

'It's the pirates!' yelled Wilbur. 'It's the pirates!'

Otter, Mr and Mrs Rat, and Ms Badger jumped down.

'Pirates?' Ms Badger smiled. 'We're not pirates. We're

just back from a lovely trip on Otter's boat.'

The Chief Weasel glowered at her. 'Then why are you wearing an eyepatch?'

Ms Badger's paw flew to her face. 'Oh, doctor's orders. I have an eye infection.'

The Chief Weasel's eyes flicked from Mr Toad, to Otter and Ms Badger. 'Something fishy's going on here.'

'The only fishy thing around here,' said Otter, 'is why there are barge-loads of trees on my river. Where did they all come from? Eh?'

The Chief Weasel hesitated. 'I don't know what you're talking about. I've never seen these barges before. Wildwood Industrious is here to give Mr Toad his prize for winning our treasure hunt.' He smiled, toothily. 'So you can't blame the trees on us, Otter.'

'Oh no,' Teejay whispered. 'They're going to get away with it!'

But Mr Rat stepped forward. 'And what is your prize, Mr Toad?' he asked. 'Because I have a feeling it could be *really* expensive.

Don't you think?'

Mr Toad looked at Mr Rat. Then he chuckled. 'Oh yes, it certainly is! It's very, *very* expensive indeed. Isn't it, Chief Weasel?' The smile fell from the Chief Weasel's face. 'For a start, it's a brand-new rowing boat,' said Mr Toad.

'A brand-new *what*? Now you listen to me, Toady—' began the Chief Weasel. But Mr Ripton whispered in his ear. The Chief Weasel scowled. 'Yes. That's right. A brand-new rowing boat.'

'Top of the range, and very costly,' said Mr Toad. 'And then, of course, a picnic hamper filled with the most delectable food. Caviar, champagne, and all that. So expensive. Very generous of the Chief Weasel.'

The Chief Weasel ground his teeth. 'All right, Toady. Have it your way. A boat and a picnic basket.'

'Excellent fellow. A damp weasel's an amenable weasel, that's what I say,' said Mr

Toad. 'And since nobody knows who owns the barges, they'll have to stay here too.'

'*What?*' roared the Chief Weasel. 'But that's—' .

'No buts,' growled Otter. 'The barges stay. Unless you want to admit to owning them?'

The Chief Weasel scowled, and shook his head.

'Thought not.' Otter went nose to nose with the Chief Weasel. 'And if I ever find dead trees on my river again, you'll have more than Mr Toad to worry about. Understood?'

The Chief Weasel glared at them all.

'I'll be back for my boat,' he snarled. 'Enjoy your prizes while you can. One day Wildwood Industrious will leave all of you high and dry!'

He stomped off up Toad Hall's lawn. Mr Ripton picked up his briefcase and followed, leading a line of soggy weasels up the grass and away.

Chapter 18
A Terrestrial Toad

Mr Toad watched them go. Then he turned and clasped his hands. 'My dear friends,' he murmured. 'And you dear, wonderful children. I'm so terribly, terribly sorry. I don't deserve the loyalty you have shown me.' Mr Toad gave a loud sniff and looked at Mr and Mrs Rat. 'I hope you'll accept the new boat from me as an apology?'

'Oh yes. Thank you!' said Mrs Rat.

'And you, Ms Badger, will you take the hamper with my fondest wishes?' said Mr Toad.

'Absolutely,' smiled Ms Badger.

'What about the barges?' said Teejay.

'I'll take those. They'll be put to a good use,' said Otter. 'Now, Toad, there's no harm done, but in future leave the river to the water folk, eh?'

'Of course. My riparian antics are at an end. I shall be a terrestrial Toad,' said Mr Toad, humbly. 'And now I would be honoured if you would join me for cream teas at Toad Hall.'

'First sensible thing you've said all week!' said Otter.

'Aaar!' cried Mr Rat. 'We have an accord!'

'I don't think pirates drink tea, dear,' said Mrs Rat.

Mr Toad led the way up to the house. As they walked, Ms Badger rummaged in a pocket, and pulled out a piece of paper.

'What's that?' said Ratty.

'I made a list of everything Mr Toad can't do any more.' Ms Badger took a pencil and wrote the word 'boats' in big letters at the bottom.

...ings Toad must not
...o ever again.
DRIVE - cars
- buses
- trains
- BOAT

Mr Toad sighed. 'So it
truly is farewell to boats,
then.' He nodded, sadly. 'I
suppose it's for the best. But
being stuck on land will be
so terribly dull.'

'You don't have to be on land,' said Mo. 'Everyone forgets you can be under it too!'

'Underground?' said Mr Toad. 'Are there really things to do down there?'

'Oh yes,' said Mo, 'all sorts! There's potholing and *mmmppffff!*'

Ratty clamped a hand over Mo's mouth. But it was too late.

Mr Toad's fingers twitched. 'Potholing? You know, that sounds as though it could be rather fun.' He peered at Ms Badger's paper. 'And it must be all right. I mean, it's not on the list or anything, is it?'

Ms Badger gave Mr Toad a hard look. 'No. It isn't.'

'But it will be,' grinned Teejay. 'It's only a matter of time.'

The End
   (It never failed to have its full effect.
51° 45 '21" N 1° 14' 51" W)

A note on Mr Toad's Mystery Co-ordinates

If you have sharp eyes you will have spotted that all the clues Mr Toad has been following have co-ordinates. And you might be wondering what happens if you try to find those co-ordinates in real life*. Well the answer to your question is this:

There's nothing stopping you from finding out!

So put on your detective's hat, and get to work. You might discover, for example, that if you very *carefully* look up the co-ordinates**, that they lead to some interesting places. These locations have quite a lot to do with Kenneth Grahame and his life. And some (but not all) of them might even have been used to inspire places in *The Wind in the Willows*.

If you would like to visit the real-world places

(with a willing grown-up or two) it could make a fun day out. But bear in mind that some of the buildings and grounds might be owned by people who live or work there—remember to keep to footpaths and public rights of way, and don't disturb anyone if you do go for a look.

Happy sleuthing, and have fun!

Tom Moorhouse

*By 'real life' I mean the places you can go in the world outside of the story. Teejay, Mr Toad, Ms Badger, and all the river folk live in a place we can only visit in books. It has its own rules and things work a bit differently there. So don't expect all of the clues to be next to a river in the real world!

**Ask a grown-up for help looking them up on one of those dumb-pewter things (as Mr Toad calls computers). Tell them to search using something that rhymes with 'frugal taps' or 'goo-gull naps', and to type in only the numbers, spaces, and letters. You can leave out the funny symbols. So, for example, 51° 33' 50" N 0° 45' 17" W can be 51 33 50 N 0 45 17 W.

The Wind in the Willows

The River Thames

Kenneth Grahame is the author of *The Wind in the Willows*, the book which has introduced generations of children to Mr Toad and his friends. Kenneth Grahame was born in 1859 and spent much of his childhood exploring the idyllic countryside along the banks of the River Thames and discovering its wildlife.

A water vole

Kenneth Grahame

After leaving school he began a career in the Bank of England. He married Elspeth Thomson in 1899 and they had a son, Alastair. When Alastair was about four years old, Kenneth Grahame began telling him bedtime stories that were to form the beginnings of *The Wind in the Willows*. The book was published in 1908 and has been loved by readers ever since.

Return to the River

Later in his life, after a period living in London and Blewbury, and after he had written his classic story for children, Grahame settled in the riverside village of Pangbourne.

Perhaps he wanted to be close to the water again? And to the places that inspired him to imagine the Wild Wood and Toad Hall?

The River Thames at Pangbourne

A note from Tom Moorhouse

OH my goodness! It's now the *third* book of Teejay's adventures with Mr Toad. This one was a joy to write, because it brought everyone

to the river and meant that I could write some new characters. And my favourite is Otter. I have spent a lot of time working by rivers, and Otter is a mixture of the folks I met there. People who live by water are a bit like rivers themselves: they can be peaceable and tranquil, stern and playful, and full of wise, mysterious depths. Otter is one of them: he's gruff, no-nonsense, and looks after everyone. I loved watching him argue with Mr Toad, who is full of nonsense, never gruff, and can't even look after himself. In short, I really enjoyed writing this book. And I hope you enjoyed reading it too!

A note from Holly Swain

Growing up I knew I wanted to do something with drawing, but I also had two other ambitions. One was to own a candyfloss-making machine (fascinating to watch and very tasty to eat!) and the other was to have a rowing boat. I'd been out in a rowing boat as a child and was mesmerised by the water weed and the little fishes darting about. I thought it was magical.

Fortunately I no longer dream of a candyfloss machine but I still love to mess about on the water. (Although it's more likely to be the sea than a river . . .)

I've really enjoyed drawing the characters in this nautical story!

If you'd like to read the original story, we have these editions available.